Emma's Very Busy Week

Written by Heather Dakota
Illustrated and designed by: Nancy Panaccione

Copyright© 2009 Scholastic Inc.

Tangerine Press
an imprint of
■ SCHOLASTIC
www.scholastic.com

Scholastic and Tangerine Press and associated logos are trademarks of Scholastic Inc

Published by Tangerine Press, an imprint of Scholastic Inc.; 557 Broadway; New York, NY 10012

10 9 8 7 6 5 4 3 2 1

ISBN-10: 0-545-17227-6
ISBN-13: 978-0-545-17227-1

Printed and bound in China

Emma has a very busy week.

She has so much to do...
school,
soccer,
ballet,
and a stack of books
from the library
to read!

Emma has ballet class
after school on Monday.

She wears her pink ballet
shoes.

Emma whirls and twirls on her toes. She loves ballet.

Emma loves reading about ballerinas, too.

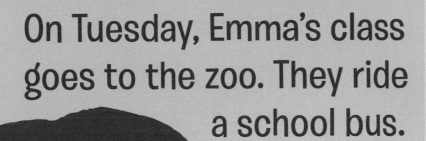

On Tuesday, Emma's class goes to the zoo. They ride a school bus.

Everyone is shouting and laughing.

Emma sees elephants,
tigers, and monkeys.
She likes the lions best.
Roar!

Before bed, Emma reads a book about wild animals.

Emma goes to Katie's house
on Wednesday.

She wants to see Katie's new puppy, Angel.

Katie, Emma, and Angel
play dress-up.

They play hide and seek, too.
Angel is good at finding them!

Emma has so much fun
with Katie and Angel.

Emma gets a kiss from Angel, too!

That night, Emma reads
a book about
puppies.

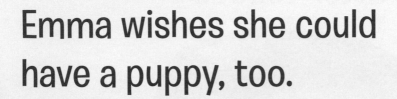

Emma wishes she could
have a puppy, too.

On Thursday, Emma's grandmother picks her up after school.

Emma gives Grandma
a big hug.

Emma and her
grandmother talk
and bake cookies. Yum!

Emma looks through the
cookbook. She looks for
cookies they can make
next week.

It is Friday! Katie spends
the night at Emma's house.

Emma and Katie watch
movies. They eat a lot
of popcorn.

The girls go to bed early.
Emma has a soccer game
in the morning.

But first, they read a scary story under the covers!

Emma plays a big soccer
game on Saturday.
Everyone claps when her
team comes out!
Emma makes a goal!
"Hooray!" everyone shouts.

That night, Emma
reads about famous
soccer players.

Emma and her family
go to the library
on Sunday.

LIBR

30

Emma has fun picking new books to read next week!